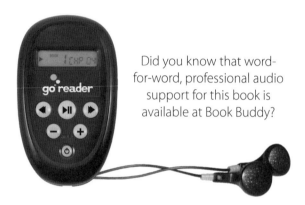

Did you know that word-for-word, professional audio support for this book is available at Book Buddy?

GoReader™ powered by Book Buddy is pre-loaded with word-for-word audio support to build strong readers and achieve Common Core standards.

The corresponding GoReader™ for this book can be found at: http://bookbuddyaudio.com

Or send an email to: info@bookbuddyaudio.com

TALES OF
THE UNCOOL

Tina Leen
the Drama Queen

BY KIRSTEN RUE
ILLUSTRATED BY SARA RADKA

Tina Leen: The Drama Queen
Tales of the Uncool

Copyright © 2015

Published by Scobre Educational

Written by Kirsten Rue

Illustrated by Sara Radka

Printed in the United States of America.

Scobre Educational
2255 Calle Clara
La Jolla, CA 92037

Scobre Operations & Administration
42982 Osgood Road
Fremont, CA 94539

www.scobre.com
info@scobre.com

Scobre Educational publications may be purchased for educational, business, or sales promotional use.

Cover and layout design by Jana Ramsay
Copyedited by Renae Reed

ISBN: 978-1-62920-134-4 (Soft Cover)
ISBN: 978-1-62920-133-7 (Library Bound)
ISBN: 978-1-62920-132-0 (eBook)

Table of Contents

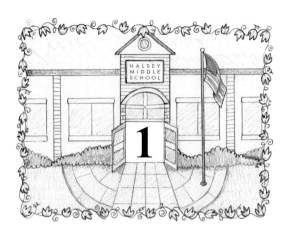

Stealing the Show

So, *it's happening. It's happening!*

These are the exact words in my head. Except I think them like I always think words: blown up in curlicue script, racing across the bottom of a television screen. I see them like the subtitles of the weirdo movies my mom watches at night when I am supposed to be sleeping.

Tina Leen, this is happening to you.

Yep. Copy that. I know it's happening because I can feel it. I am standing up during a "Playing is Learning" summer camp talent show spectacular, sponsored by Freeburger. I'm supposed to play the part of a dancing low-cal milkshake and do what the script calls a "shimmy shake." I am supposed to do that, on stage, and then wink and smile at all the parents and other kids in the audience and say, "Free to be fat-free!" at the end. I know my mom's out there. She's probably rolling her eyes and poking her friend Maeve and clucking "So corporate" in her disapproving voice.

And I know that Stella Sweet, the unofficial boss of camp, is staring at me from offstage, because I can *feel* that, too. It's like if the light over a dentist's chair and the sting of a sunburn teamed up to zap me with the Glare of Doom. Ouch.

Yet, *it's happening.* I can't stop it. And the next thing I know I'm laid out, arms out to either side, staring at little puffs of cloud. They float past, all *chugga-choo-choo.* Mr. Diavolo, my old art teacher turned drama coach, is fanning me with a program. I can hear my mom's concerned voice in the crowd, and Stella?

She comes over and rips off the foam headband I'm wearing, her lips all pursed up in a scowl. "Ruined!" she hisses.

"Hey!" I mumble, even though I know she's already stormed away. "That headband was supposed to be my straw!"

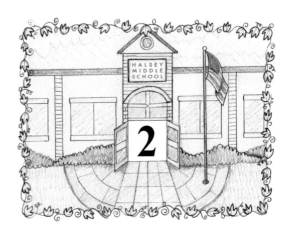

Forced Agreement

I HAVE WHAT THE DOCTORS CALL VENTRICULAR DYSFUNCTION. Even after all these years, I can barely pronounce the words. It means my heart has a harder time pumping blood than other people's sometimes. Overall, it's pretty lame, and there's really no way around it. I've lost count of the times I've fainted or had to sit down, this shivery weak feeling taking over all the nerves in my hands and spine. I've learned things to avoid, though: being outside too long in the summer, standing up too fast, sprinting in gym class (*Score!*). Over the years, I became very good at avoiding anything that might bring on a fainting fit. So good that I didn't have one of my faints for a very long time.

When the summer before sixth grade started, it felt like the illness was finally under my control. I tried taking deep breaths, like my doctor said, whenever my body seemed shaky. I even ate more "healthy" things (also his idea). All in all, I felt like a brand-new girl, right out of the box. At first, I planned just to sit in the pottery room during "Playing is Learning," making a coil pot. You make them by slowly notching each little tube of wet clay with a fork and then even more slowly aligning each circle of clay with the one under it. But the thing is, the heat from outside kept belching into the art room. I could hear the other kids out there laughing and practicing lines and turning on music from someone's phone.

It took me a while to realize it, but then it came to me: I wanted to be in the talent show myself. Pretty badly. Of course, if I had known that my ventric . . .

thing was going to rear its ugly head just in time to humiliate me in front of the entire school, I might have stopped myself. I would have told myself, "Tina, you're no actress. You're a quiet girl who faints if she smells eggs and is supposed to be making coil pots in the pottery room." But, that warning never came. And even if it had, I might have brushed right past, nose thrust up in the air, and ignored it. For once, I wanted to believe I could be a different Tina Leen. Just for once, I wanted to be in the middle of something, with people clapping for Tina Leen the Drama Queen. Sure, my mom sometimes calls me a Drama Queen when I stamp my feet and complain in the supermarket, but I mean a *real* Drama Queen. The kind who makes everybody stop and listen. That's kinda my dream. So sue me.

But, now, on the first day back at Halsey for sixth grade, I'm not exactly trying to make eye contact with anyone as I step off the bus. Sure, it's been two weeks, but I *know* other kids are going to remember the pageant. Trust me: I don't need that kind of

attention. I lean in for the long march between the curb
and the front doors, which are already smeared with
fingerprints. In fact, I keep my head so low, my hair
so in front of my eyes, and my backpack so tucked in
front of my stomach that I don't even see that a boy is
opening the door for me.

"Um, hey! Tina?"

It's a boy I don't even recognize with jagged dark
hair over his eyes and slumped, rounded shoulders.

"The fry in the back," he says.

"What?" Have Stella and the Sweets invented a new cool word? It's so easy to get behind.

"I was the fry in the back—remember? I was supposed to do the shimmy shake next to you. During the show."

Then it hits me: This boy saw My Most Embarrassing Moment on stage. I eye him from underneath my hair. I don't know what it is about hair. It just feels like an extra layer of protection. I've been told it's super emo, but then I've also been called *Spoon Face* by some of the cool girls, so I'd say the messages are pretty mixed.

"Um, yeah?" I tense, ready to make a quick exit in case this guy is about to make me a punchline.

But all he asks is if I'm okay. Barely inside the doors of the school, and someone—someone I don't even know—actually cares? Maybe things at Halsey will be different this year.

———

FLASH FORWARD TO LUNCHTIME, THOUGH, AND I REALIZE I've been far too quick with that thought. I don't have extra money for the pizza line, so I'm peeling a totally gross slab of "BBQ beef" from the top of the stack. Just then, I hear my name from a table across the room.

"Tina Leen!"

It's my name, alright, sneered through the lipgloss-decked lips of Stella Sweet, just the person you *don't* want to notice you. I flip the hair from my eyes and look over at a table of giggling girls: the Sweets. They come in all flavors of thin, pretty, and shiny-nailed. Their hair is neatly scooped back into ponytails that bounce like perfectly curved commas. They are my worst nightmare.

"Tina!" Stella says again, waving at me. "Come over here. I need you to settle a question for me."

Although it occurs to me to drop my tray and make a run for the first-floor bathroom, there's something about Stella's voice that makes her seem like a scary principal you wouldn't dare to disobey. So, slowly, worried I might faint all over again, I inch over to the table.

"Take your time," she says as I shuffle across the room, "All that forehead must really keep you weighed down." The other Sweets snicker.

She gestures to an empty seat when I've arrived and says, in a voice dripping with fake phone niceness, "Please sit down." What can I do except take a seat? When Stella makes a request, you jump.

She looks over her can of Diet Coke at me, twirling it in her palms. "So," she says. "Fainting is kind of your thing, isn't it?"

"Um . . ." I say, too embarrassed to meet her eyes or the eyes of the other girls peering at me as if I were a science project.

"You can, like, drop on command. I mean, everyone knew you had the *stupidest* part in the talent show. So I know what you did." She puts her face so close to me that I can smell the lipgloss she wears; it smells like a cross between bubblegum and a watermelon Jolly

Rancher. "You got out of it," she whispers.

"Well, actually—" I say, about to explain about my weak heart and how sometimes it runs out of blood, leaving me to sway and watch the world dimpling with globs of light before everything goes black.

Stella stops me. "Seems like something you can teach," she says. "And I could use that skill. To get out of gym. And, you know, whatever it is I don't feel like doing." Behind her, the rest of the Sweets are bobble-heading in agreement.

"Deal?" she says, holding out her hand. The lunch bell starts ringing right as she mashes my sweaty fingers between her own. By the time I'm ready to say no, explain that actually I'm *sick*, not just fainting for fun, the Sweets are gone. It's just me and the cold Play-Doh of the BBQ beef on my plate. Across the room, I spot that boy from the front door earlier. He waves.

Great. What a day.

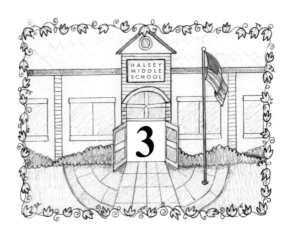

One Speaker

I FINALLY LEARN THE BOY'S NAME DURING THE LAST CLASS of the day. And what, you might ask, is the last class of the day? Drama. I know. What kind of bizarre brain fart could possibly have led me to sign up for *drama*? Especially after my fainting incident in front of the entire school, including the drama teacher himself? Well, it came down to three things:

One, Mr. Diavolo was my favorite teacher last year, and he switched from teaching art to drama. I wanted to see him jiggle his spidery eyebrows for one last class and hear him singing weirdo operas to himself while we bent over our glitter glue. *Two*, we signed up for classes *before* the talent show. *Three* . . . Stupidity. Beyond that, it's a mystery. Now, Mr. Diavolo jiggles his eyebrows and hums to himself while handing out thin little books. *Famous Monologues of History*, the book is called. Just then I notice that that boy is sitting next to me. He smiles shyly and raises his eyebrows, as if to say "What the heck is this?"

I can't help myself and smile back.

"Monologues!" Mr. Diavolo begins, dancing back and forth on his feet. "From the Greek term for 'one logic' . . . or one voice . . . or ONE! One person! Speaking! Thrilling! Gesturing! Roping the audience into her thrall! Keeping butts on the edges of their seats! Bringing down the house!" Mr. Diavolo has both arms raised above his head, like he's waiting for someone to drop something into his arms from the sky.

"By the end of this class on December 15th, you will all have chosen, *memorized*, and performed a

monologue for the entire sixth grade. You will have joined the greatest theatrical tradition of all time!" Mr. Diavolo's voice booms so loudly that I can see Ms. Arple from across the hall, pulling down the shade on her front door and shaking her head. "You will have drunk from the cup of glory and become like the Greeks! Like Hamlet! Like, I don't know, some actor from your favorite TV show! You will do this, or what can I say, you just might not pass this class."

I mean, I'm not making it up. Who would want to miss a teacher making this kind of speech? Mr. Diavolo can make desks shake with his voice and get even Stella Sweet to stop chewing her gum. Except then it hits me. Perform? By myself? On stage? In front of everyone? Or FAIL?!? I lean forward and let my hair fall over my face. I run it through in my head: How bad is failing a class, really? Could I get a doctor's note? What would Mom say if I came home with a big fat "F" on my report card?

Tina Leen, Drama Queen?

More like, Tina Leen, Fainting Queen.

"Hey," the boy next to me taps me on the shoulder. "We're supposed to partner up and practice the lines the teacher wrote on the board. Wanna be mine?"

"Sure," I say, though truthfully my thoughts are like a non-stop train that's headed for a big crash somewhere between PANIC and FEAR.

"I'm Julian," he says, and shakes my hand. My second handshake of the day, I realize, and it makes me remember something. Something about practicing for the talent show, and there being a boy with a really high, really pretty voice. That was Julian. One of the other boys kept calling him Madonna because of his nice voice.

"Hey Madonna!" the boy would shout, "Shouldn't you be standing with the other girls?"

I blush, embarrassed by the memory and for Julian. It seems like we're sort of in the same boat. Despised, disliked, and very, *very* uncool.

I take a deep breath and lean in closer. Here goes

nothing! "Julian," I whisper. "I don't know what I'm going to do. I can't do this monologue thing. I *can't*. And to top it off, Stella Sweet wants me to teach her how to faint whenever she wants. She made me promise. What am I going to do?"

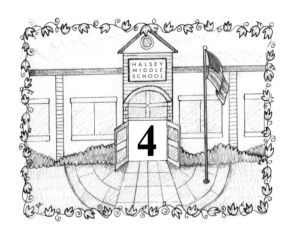

Choices

ONE MONTH AFTER THE FIRST DAY OF SCHOOL, MY problems aren't exactly solved. I wake up each morning and try not to make eye contact with myself in the mirror while brushing my teeth. Once, I did that and fainted out of nowhere. So, clearly, I freak MYSELF out. Then, I head for the bus. As I step through the folding doors of the bus, I'm welcomed by that familiar bus smell of rotting peach, pencil erasers, and jacket sweat. If that doesn't make the day seem depressing, I don't know what does. The one good thing is that I know Julian will be waiting at the school doors for me. I don't know how this became our tradition, exactly, but it just seems like he's there every day with a grin on his face. After a couple of weeks of this, I started to grin, too, when I saw him. Sometimes I even bring a little baggie with extra Oreos from home to share with him. I'll hold one side of the cookie and he'll hold the other and we practice twisting them apart like they do in commercials. So far, I'd say our success rate is one in three.

To get us through the rest of the school day, Julian and I have made up a little routine we call the Sweet Check. Even if Stella and her crew of girls barely know he exists, Julian is nice enough to help me avoid them. When we do a Sweet Check, I'll open my locker and then look into it really hard like I'm trying not to forget something. Meanwhile, Julian will creep over to the cafeteria doors and make a scan. If he sees no evidence of the Sweets, he'll look over at me and make the "OK" sign. If they're there, we go to the library, wait until the last possible second, and then rush in at the very end of lunch hour. We pile food onto our plates and try to eat it as quickly as we can before the bell rings.

———

I THINK MR. DIAVOLO IS ON TO US, THOUGH. LAST WEEK, we were using teamwork to fill our lunch trays. I ordered Julian "Meat!" and he ordered back "Salad!" We both tried to get our trays filled up in record time. Mr. Diavolo smiled at us from his watching position as lunch monitor. I swear that one of his eyebrows jumped up from his forehead and practically did a handstand.

"For whom the bell tolls," he chuckled as the bell started to ring. Julian and I moaned and started walking to the check-out line. "How are those monologues coming along, you two? Have you picked your big speeches yet?"

"What?" I asked, hoping to put him off.

"One actor, alone on stage. It will be marvelous! You will take the audience to places they've never been before! Your voice will create a magic world of the imagination! With only one chance to succeed!"

Gulp. As if I needed another reminder! With that, Mr. Diavolo walked away.

"Man," Julian said, "That guy is the weirdest teacher I've ever had."

LATER, AS JULIAN AND I MET UP BETWEEN BELLS, HE ASKED me why I was so afraid of the drama class final.

"Julian," I hissed, "did you not *see* the big fat fainting show I made as soon as it was my turn to act in the pageant?"

Julian's face was its normal calm. You can get mad and cranky, but whatever you do, his face stays like the same smooth, clear lake. He's just a chill guy, I guess. "Well, I saw you in rehearsals. You were . . . *good.*"

"Nuh uh."

"Yeah, you were. I thought you were."

"Well, um, that's nice and all, but don't you think you're kinda biased?"

"Maybe," Julian said, "but there's this and avoiding Stella and I dunno, all these other things you do. Maybe there can be a better way of, I guess, not avoiding stuff."

Out of nowhere, I felt the weak sensation of a fainting fit coming on. It felt like extra air had been injected into the space between my bones, and I was about to drift away.

"Uh oh." I whispered to him. "Don't make anyone notice us, but I need to go to the nurse and lie down. *NOW.*" Julian hurried to put his hand under my arm. Conversation: closed.

As we walked slowly down the hall, I heard Stella's voice above the sound of lockers closing and the blippity bloops of cellphone games.

"I see what you're doing, Tina! Getting out of class! Don't forget our little dealiooooooo!" She said the last part in this high, sing-song voice. Even after a month passing, she hadn't forgotten about the "deal" she'd made with me in the lunchroom. Like I could just teach her to do what was happening to me now. It was all a game to Stella Sweet, even if it wasn't a game to me.

WITH JUST A MONTH AND A HALF TO GO BEFORE MONOLOGUE Day, I'm reading in my favorite place in the house. I read with my back and head on the couch cushions and my feet propped over the back. Whenever I get to a hard part in my book, I like to make a little twirl with my foot. Left, right, left, right. This book is *Famous*

Monologues of History from drama class, and let's just say I'm doing a lot of foot twirling. I've been skimming through it for what feels like *hours*. Still, I haven't found a single monologue that I can even imagine saying out loud with a huge crowd sitting in front of me. Here's what some of the speeches are like . . .

"It was the best of times, it was the worst of times . . ." Or, just the worst of times.

"To be or not to be . . ." I'll take "not being" rather than finish this speech, thanks.

I can't even get through the rest of the speeches. I have no idea what the speakers are trying to say!

I start to be distracted by the smell of a stir-fry my mom is making in the kitchen. Each slice of pepper she drops in the pan makes a sizzling sound.

"Mom! You're killing me with that!"

"What?" she says.

"You're being so LOUD!" I yell back, although I know it's not the peppers, or Mom, that's frustrating me.

"Well, that's funny, coming from someone who

loves blasting the TV," she chuckles. "What's got you all wound up?"

"Stupid mono-*whatevers* for stupid drama class." I pout.

Mom leaves the kitchen, wiping her hands on a towel, and comes to hover over me and my book. "That one," she says, stabbing her finger into the open index section of my book. "Why not do that one? You loved that movie when you were a kid." With that, she's back to dropping things into the stir-fry pan.

Reluctantly, I look at the monologue Mom has chosen. *Alice in Wonderland.* Hmmmm. For some reason I never imagined it would be okay to choose a speech from a cartoon girl in a cartoon movie who talks to rabbits and cats. I mean, there are so many *serious* and *important* monologues in the book. But there's her name—Alice—right there. And Mr. Diavolo *said* we could choose any monologue in the book.

Hmmmmmmmm. . . .

HALSEY MIDDLE SCHOOL

5

Far to Fall

COUNTDOWN TO MONOLOGUE DAY:
3 WEEKS, 2 DAYS, 10 HOURS

"So. I've heard rumors." Stella has cornered me out of nowhere as I'm flipping through the original chapter book of *Alice in Wonderland* in the library. I guess it's impossible even to read without being watched in this school.

"I have Mr. Diavolo, too. Second period."

"Um, hum." *Keep your head down, Tina. Don't let*

her remember about the fainting pact!

"Looks like we're doing the *same* piece."

"What?" I'm genuinely surprised. Stella's white teeth—small and sharp—glisten behind her lips.

"Two Alices. And you're not even blonde. I hope you know what you're getting into, Tina." Stella leans in and pokes me with a long pink nail. I'm pretty sure it's fake, because no real nail could be that long and square. At least, not mine, which are all torn up and covered with ink stains.

"I didn't do it on purpose," I squeak.

"Sure. Sure you didn't."

"I didn't!"

"Well, all I'm saying is—" *Please don't mention the weird fainting thing, please don't mention the weird fainting thing . . .*

"—if you want to avoid some trouble, I would remember our little deal. I'm bored of math class and stuff. You share your secrets, and then it's just *Pop!* and I can go home sick. And who knows, maybe a handsome eighth grader will catch me when I fall." She smirks and pretends to collapse, her hand dramatically pressed to her forehead. *D'oh!* At this point, I'm practically as flat as a book on the shelf myself, leaning back as far as I can to get away from Stella. I can barely breathe. Her hair is blinding me with its shine and she smells like bubblegum and fruit and sparkles (if sparkles can have a smell, that is). Stella grins, gives a little shake of her head, and is gone. She strides just like a queen to the library doors.

Well, this is it. Stella keeps insisting that I teach her something that's unteachable. I'm officially screwed.

"I GUESS I HAVE TO CHANGE MY PIECE THEN," I SAY TO Julian over lunch, glumly moving my limp salad leaves around the plate.

"Why? I don't get it."

"BeCAUSE. Isn't it obvious?"

"Not to me, no."

"I do my piece. She does something mean back.

Something I probably haven't even *imagined* yet. OR, I pretend like I can teach her to faint so she doesn't ruin my piece. But then she realizes that I *can't* teach her that, because it's not something I can just *control*. And she still does something mean." I put my head to the table and groan.

Julian doesn't seem to have much pity for me today, though. He's just quiet, thinking about things, tilting his head a little bit to the side.

"But you've practiced it. We've been practicing them for weeks now."

"Well, I'll just have to practice a new one." I slide the gross salad away from myself so it can't make me even sadder than I already am.

Julian is still thinking. "I just wouldn't accept it, you know?" he bursts out, almost like he's mad at me. "I just wouldn't act so, so *defeated*. Before you've even tried."

Oh great, so now my best friend isn't even on my side. *Best friend.* It's just now, as he's kind of yelling at me, that I realize this is the truth. Julian. Me. Best friends. Except at this very moment he's clearing up his chip bag and tray and not even taking the Oreos I brought specially for him. A flare of anger rises up in me. He can't just leave!

"Oh, this is great," I yell. "You want me to just, I dunno, get OVER it, but it's not like YOU'RE trying to be a singer. It's not like it was so easy to just forget all those mean boys at summer camp! What did they call you again? *Madonna?*"

As soon as the words come out of my mouth, I wish I could reverse time for one minute and erase them. Julian's cheeks go red, and he stands there for a moment holding his lunch tray like a shield in front of him. Then, without another word, he storms off. What just happened?! Are we actually in a real, live fight?

Now, it is *never* a good idea to cry in Halsey School. It's like there's a Cry Cam hidden up somewhere in the rafters and the minute you show weakness, it's broadcast all over the school. People will start calling

you a cry baby in the halls. Believe me, I know this. Even so, I let just one tear squeeze out and curve down my cheek. It lands on the table and starts puddling towards the salad. They're a match made in heaven.

———————

LATER THAT DAY IN MR. DIAVOLO'S CLASS, JULIAN WON'T even sit by me. I'm left sitting at one of the reject desks. They're always broken, and this one is no exception. Plus, someone has carved *Halsey Eats Souls* in all caps into its hard surface. Tell me about it, Desk. We're supposed to be having quiet memorization time, and I'm bent over my book. The familiar words of Alice's monologue are in front of me. She's following the White Rabbit down the rabbit hole, but naturally she's afraid because, well:

One, he's a talking rabbit. And that's weird.

Two, hitting the bottom of the rabbit hole is really going to hurt her butt when she lands.

Three, she doesn't actually know how long the rabbit hole is, or how far she has left to fall. That makes it even scarier.

"After such a fall as this, I shall think nothing of tumbling down stairs. How brave they'll all think me at home," she says.

I glance over at Julian, but he's curled so far over his book that his hair is making a curtain over his face. He totally learned that from me. I push some over my own eyes, too. Even if he *does* look over, he won't be able to see my face, either. I know I should be looking through the monologue book. I should be finding a new monologue to memorize at the last minute, but I feel stuck just where Alice is stuck. How far do I have left to fall, and how hard is it going to hurt when I hit the real bottom? Halsey School has never felt so hopeless.

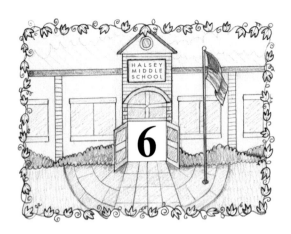

Down the Rabbit Hole

"NO CHANGES, NO SUBSTITUTIONS, NO RETURNS." MR. Diavolo says. I've cornered him just a few days before we are supposed to perform our monologues during the gigantoid school assembly. I asked him really nicely if I could switch monologues to this one about Juliet loving Romeo and wanting to rename a rose. I guess I'm not one of his favorite students after all, though. All of those eyebrow jiggles were one big fake. He says no, I have to do my original piece. He might as well be saying, "Tina Leen, I don't even care if you drop dead." I *will* be dead after I perform this piece. Stella will be glaring at me from the sidelines, and what— What if I faint? *Again?* In front of everyone?! It feels like I can't breathe.

"You're ruining my life, Mr. Diavolo!" I stamp my foot for good measure.

"Tina, that's just the sort of big drama I'm looking for." He pats me on the shoulder, smiles, and walks away. Like a reflex, I look over towards Julian, who is gathering his bag across the room. I got so used to looking over and raising my eyebrows at him during class and seeing him grin in return. It's a fresh sting each time I look over now and he doesn't even notice. Each time, I remember saying, *"What did they call you again? Madonna?"* in my rudest voice. No wonder he hates me now.

If he would only look over at me, maybe I could

somehow make a face that says, *"I'm sorry!"* I never meant to say that—it was like an Evil Tina Leen took over for just that moment. It wasn't the real me. And when I emerge on the other side of whatever's going to happen during Monologue Day, it sure would be nice to have a friend.

THE NIGHT BEFORE MONOLOGUE DAY IS SPAGHETTI NIGHT, but I'm so nervous about tomorrow that I can barely eat a bite. I know Mom thinks that's weird, because usually I slurp up spaghetti like a vacuum slurps up dust. Bad feelings have been with me all day. Sometimes I feel like I'm going to float away, and other times I feel like a hot stone is burning in my stomach. As much as I want to eat the spaghetti on my plate, that hot stone is just not letting me.

"Tina," Mom says. "What's up? You're not eating; you've got your hair all covering your face. What's going on with you?"

"Mo-om, I'm fine," I growl back, staring at my

plate like I can read my spaghetti. Those tears I've been holding back every day at Halsey School have decided that now is the perfect time for them to take the stage.

"And what about your friend? Julian? I haven't heard you mention him lately."

That's it! The floodgates are open; the dam is broken. Whatever you want to call it, I am crying for real. My own sobs sound so loud that I almost feel like I'm a character in a movie, crying for a big audience. I don't really like being this kind of Drama Queen.

Mom pats my head. "Sweetie, what is it?"

"Can I please be excused from school tomorrow? I'm sick. I mean—I'm not sick now—but I *will* be. Or possibly dead."

"Oh. OH!" Mom thunks her forehead with her palm. "It's your drama class. And what happened at the summer camp pageant."

"No doy, Mom!"

"Well, sweetheart," she says, reaching over to

squeeze my arm, "I know this sounds like a cop-out, but sometimes you have to do the things that scare you the most, just so you know you can."

"Thanks, Mom. Thanks a LOT. Now I feel so much better. NOT!"

"Well, I know it's annoying, but there it is."

I sigh as heavily as I can, but I know I'm out of luck. It's like Mom and Mr. Diavolo have made a pact to show absolutely no sympathy for my problems. Thanks, Tina Leen's Life Ruiners.

But my mom's not done with the amazing advice yet. "Have you tried just talking to him? To your friend?"

Sometimes moms can be so clueless.

———————

THE NEXT DAY—MONOLOGUE DAY—I HAVE TO DASH OUT of homeroom and run to the bathroom because I'm so sure I'm going to throw up. *Tina, meet toilet.* I stare at the toilet bowl until I feel calm enough to take some deep, cool breaths. Slowly, the nausea goes away and it's just back to the familiar dread with no possibility of upchuck. Okay. At least I won this round.

I get ready to peel myself off the cold tile floor and head back to class. Just then, the bathroom door swings open. From my position on the stall floor, I can see two neat little pink-sneakered feet strolling in. On each lace sits a little sparkly sticker in the shape of a heart: the classic signature of the Sweets. Pink Shoes is followed by Teal Shoes is followed by Yellow Shoes. Three sets of sparkly heart stickers. Three sets

of matchy shoes lined up in front of where the mirrors and sinks are.

"Stella, don't even worry. You're obviously going to be the best," says Yellow Shoes.

"Oh, yeah, like, um, no contested or contestants or whatever," Teal Shoes agrees.

Stella (*a.k.a. Pink Shoes. Of course.*) sighs heavily. "Well, I've been kind of thinking about acting in commercials. Like that girl who goes to Jefferson West and got to jump up and down in the Freeburger commercials."

"Oh, yeah," Yellow and Teal agree with admiration.

"I mean, every star has to start somewhere. Like even Selena Gomez had to start *somewhere.*"

"Totally."

"But I mean, I wouldn't, like, let the fame go to my head or anything. I'd still totally invite you guys on my boat and stuff."

"Awwww," coo Yellow and Teal. *Are they really buying this stuff?*

"But, um, don't tell Dana. The guest list has to remain special."

This whole time my knee has been bent in a weird shape up against the stall door. I shift ever so slightly to ease the pressure. So far, I thank my lucky stars that the Sweets have obviously been looking at themselves too hard to notice my occupied stall. Then, *Clang!* I totally hit the toilet paper dispenser with my knee.

The Sweets freeze and stop talking as the *Clang!* echoes in the bathroom.

"Um, who's there?" yells Stella. I'm scrambling to my feet, but it's too late. The dreaded Pink Shoes stalks over to my stall. She bangs on the door once, twice, and then starts rattling it back and forth. The door's hinges creak and moan. Geez! I wouldn't have guessed Stella was strong enough to destroy a door, but I guess all that concentrated evil gives her super powers or something.

"Open it, or I'm breaking it down!" she shrieks. The lock looks like it's about to snap and I swear paint is chipping off the sides. Game's over. If I thought dry heaving into a grungy toilet in the sixth grade bathroom was bad, *this* is worse times, I dunno, like a zillion. Fingers trembling, I open the stall door.

"Tina Leen," Stella says, shaking her head slowly and clucking her tongue behind her teeth. "I didn't think you'd actually *spy* on me to get your way."

I don't know why I'm always so tongue-tied around Stella. I want to tell her that, no, that doesn't even make sense. Clearly I was already there before they came in. I can't get the words out, though. All I can do is stand there.

"Ha!" Stella says, spitting out the word like bad gum. "Arent'cha going to faint now?" She grins a mean grin. "I'll see YOU here tomorrow. Same time. Same place. And we can start my lessons. I've got a math test next week and your fainting trick is going to get me out of it. After all, that was our deal. ESPECIALLY since you decided to copy my skit." Teal and Yellow Shoes glare at me from behind her.

"Good luck, by the way," she says in the most sarcastic voice possible, rolling her eyes. "You're going to need it."

Then, in perfect unison, all three Sweets turn their backs and leave the room. I check my watch. Two hours 'til showtime. I guess I should enjoy my last hours of freedom.

―――――

WHEN I FINALLY EXIT THE BATHROOM AFTER MISSING the rest of homeroom, Julian is standing there. He's pretending to read a poster on the wall nearby that says "Freeburger's High Protein Zonko Bites Are Great For Growing Teens!" I'm not buying it.

"What are you doing here?" I ask, trying to sound distant and queenly, even though all I want to do is break down and cry.

"Well," Julian says, a small smile curling the edge of his lip. "I wondered if you want to run your lines in the rec yard with me. Plus, I figured you might need some backup." And with that, after three weeks of nothing, there's a truce between Julian and me. I don't exactly understand why, but let's just say I'm grateful to have my only friend back. Plus, Julian's the only person who doesn't want me to fall on my face up there on stage during my monologue.

"Cool," I say. "That sounds good."

Despite my time of doom ticking closer by the moment, I can almost feel a smile coming on. After what I said to Julian, I'm not even one hundred percent sure I deserve this.

SINCE MR. DIAVOLO WOULDN'T LET ME CHANGE MY monologue, I'm stuck gloomily reciting my *Alice in Wonderland* lines to Julian, my audience of one.

"I never realized that rabbit holes were so dark . . . and so long . . . and so empty. I believe I have been falling for five minutes, and I still can't see the bottom!"

"Um, maybe add some personality to it?" he says.

"Why? So I can sound okay right before Stella

ruins it?!" But, just for fun, I try saying the words in a few different ways and even throwing my voice to sound like I really *am* falling down a long, long tunnel. I make my voice sound fainter and fainter.

Julian laughs. "See! You're really good at this!" The bell rings and the rec yard begins to clear. I kick at a pile of leaves on the pavement.

"Julian. I'm sorry. About . . . things." *Not winning the Oscar for THIS speech.*

Julian just smiles. "It's cool. I'm . . . um . . . er . . . sorry. Too."

"We are both terrible at this." I crack a smile back.

"Pretty much." We break out laughing and for a minute I feel as if nothing has been bad about sixth grade so far. Nothing at all. Forget fainting and Stella and sitting in a bathroom stall. It hasn't been so bad. Julian and I laugh and laugh, doubled over, our elbows resting on our knees. I could almost pee my pants, I'm laughing so hard.

The second bell rings, though, cutting us short.

Now, we're part of the wave of kids in their bright coats who are flowing back to their lockers and then to classes and then . . .

And *then* . . .

To the *stage*. That moment of, *Hey, I feel great, no worries*? Yep. That's officially gone. Here we go down that dark, long tunnel.

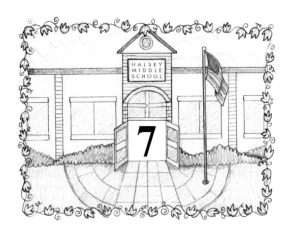

Center Stage

I'VE SEEN PLENTY OF MOVIES ABOUT KIDS PERFORMING at a school. Usually, when the kids are backstage in those films, they're always humming or singing musical scales. Usually one of them is playing a piano. Plus, there's some friendly person with a clipboard to smile at whomever's about to go on stage and whisper, "Break a leg!" Backstage at Halsey School is pretty much just Halsey School. The only difference is you have to stand in a line next to the old velvet curtains, which are dusty and make my nose tingle. We're lined up in alphabetical order. Thank goodness Julian's last name is Marcos and he's only one person away. This also means that I will be performing my monologue *before* Stella Sweet.

Mr. Diavolo is sitting out in the auditorium along with a bunch of other teachers and their classrooms. Peeking through the curtains, I see kids flicking paper wads and playing on their phones, even though the teachers keep giving them dirty looks. Pretty typical. Underneath my shirt my heart thumps so hard that I'm surprised no one can see it. It's jumping like crazy in there! My brain is swirling with thoughts. I think of *Alice in Wonderland*'s rabbit and his pocketwatch and the countdown to my monologue. I think of Stella. Under all of these thoughts is a little prayer of *"Please, whatever happens, don't let me faint."*

I picture meeting Stella in the bathrooms tomorrow

and trying to tell her about the whole fainting thing. She's not going to get over me performing the very same monologue *before* hers today, I just know it. I wonder if I *can* teach her, somehow, if I'm desperate enough. Like maybe I could Google "fainting tricks" or something on the internet. (Let's be honest, I Google "fainting" about three times a day already.) I doubt Stella would buy it, though. One thing I know about Stella: She is not dumb. Terrifying, and not the nicest tool in the shed? Definitely. But not dumb.

My mind's been racing so quickly that I don't even realize just how fast the line is moving forward. Suddenly—*way* before I'm ready—it's me waiting in the front of the line. The toes of my sneakers touch the scuffed wood floors of the small auditorium stage. My breath catches in my throat. There are a lot of kids out there, too.

The girl ahead of me stumbles through her piece, pausing a few times to look at notes that are written on her hands. Out in the audience, Mr. Diavolo wiggles an eyebrow disapprovingly and scribbles something down in his notebook. The girl ahead of me finishes and bows and gets off the stage as soon as possible. A few kids and teachers clap. Mr. Diavolo shuffles his papers.

Tick . . . Tock . . .

"Tina . . . Tina Leen! You're up next. Performing a monologue from *Alice in Wonderland.*"

Somebody squeezes my arm and says, "Break a leg!" I glance back and see Julian, smiling at me as I head forward onto the stage. Now it's just me, the spotlight, and about a hundred kids I barely know.

Tick . . . Tock . . .

COUNTDOWN: 0

NOW, HERE'S THE THING. YOU MIGHT NOT BELIEVE THAT a person can have about a hundred thoughts in only a few seconds, but I am proof that this *can* happen. As I stand there, heart *ka-thunking*, preparing to end my sad excuse for a social life by starting in on Alice's speech, I have a thought. Or, a hundred thoughts. I mean, who's counting? Me, on a stage with the entire sixth grade out there, staring at me? Well, it's sorta my nightmare. Something I have avoided since Day One. Ever since I realized I was different than the other kids and couldn't always control my own body.

I think of this morning and how I was sitting in a bathroom stall, about to throw up. I was convinced I didn't have a friend in the world because Julian and I weren't speaking to each other. It was a bad feeling. Except now the two of us *are* speaking to each other. Julian actually believes I can be a good actress, even if I don't believe it.

One, this whole time I thought I fell in a rabbit hole of my own, plunging and plunging into darkness. I wasn't sure where I was going to hit bottom, or how much it was going to hurt. But the thing I hadn't realized was this: I'd already hit the bottom. I'd been a scaredy cat of everything, to the point where I almost lost my own best friend. *That* had been the big "Ouch!" at the end of the tunnel. I already knew what that felt like. I knew what it felt like to have no friends and be afraid of everyone. And yet I had survived.

Two, if I already hit the hard rock at the bottom of the tunnel and lived to tell the tale, then nothing else could be that bad. Right? Because even if I fainted right now or Stella followed me around every day for the rest of the school year poking me in the back with a mechanical pencil, I would still have my friend, no matter what. And also, wasn't I now climbing back *up?*

Three, I'm pretty over this whole situation and ready to set the record straight, once and for all. I mean, I didn't choose to be sick. The sickness chose me. If Alice is brave enough to go somewhere new with only herself to rely on, then I am, too.

All of these thoughts gather together in my head. I take a deep breath, and instead of performing my monologue at all, this is what I say:

"Hi. My name is Tina. Tina Leen. You guys might

remember me from the pageant this summer when I fainted right in front of everybody."

I see Mr. Diavolo look up in surprise, and a few kids shift in their seats. They shrug their shoulders as if to say, *"Don't ask me! That girl's crazy!"*

I continue. "Let me explain. I don't do stuff like that on purpose. Like, not at all. It's part of something that goes on with me, that I've had since I was little. It's called ventricular dysfunction. Yeah, I know. Say that three times fast." I smile a little at my own joke, and out in the auditorium, I swear I see a couple of kids smiling back.

"All it means is that I'm a normal kid, but sometimes my heart can't keep up with me. And when it can't, lame stuff happens. Like fainting in a milkshake costume. Believe me, I hate it the most out of everyone: not being able to predict if I'll do something bizarre . . . like even faint right now! But on the other hand, it's who I am. If I went through every day of my life avoiding things thinking that I'd faint or look stupid in front of everyone, I would never get anything done. And I *do* want to do things. So. That's my story. That's my monologue. I guess I could ask you to be okay with it—with me being different—but I kinda figure that as long as I'm okay with myself, that's all that matters."

Silence.

I can't believe I just did that!!

I bow, hear a few claps, and then rush off the stage as quickly as possible. My heart is still beating hard, but in a different way than before. Right now, it feels like how I imagine it feels to run as hard and fast as I can: unstoppable. I actually feel good. I feel light. I feel like a million bucks. And for some reason, all that fear from before has just poofed away and gone to live somewhere else. Like maybe in some dark corner of the rec yard or in one of the restrooms on the fourth floor. Wherever it's gone, good riddance! I look across the stage to where Julian is still standing in line and he gives me a huge double thumbs up sign, grinning from ear to ear.

When I sit down with the rest of the class to watch the end of the drama class recital, my heart is still thumping. It all feels like a blur: the bright lights on stage and Mr. Diavolo patting me on the shoulder as I take my seat. A few other kids even smile at me from the row behind me, although the Sweets in the crowd are definitely glaring. I know Stella is still backstage and I wonder what she's thinking. Then I decide, *You know what? I don't even care.* Julian takes the stage for his monologue and I clap as hard as I can. By the time he sits down next to me, my hands are practically numb. The two of us smile at each other, and Julian pulls a celebratory Oreo out of his pocket. We twist it apart—perfectly—and clink our two halves together like parents do with wine glasses.

"Stella Sweet!" Mr. Diavolo calls out.

There's a pause and then Stella walks out. She seems to be scanning the crowd, looking for someone.

It's me, I realize as she catches my eye and nods, just ever so slightly. I nod back. I guess when you're Stella Sweet, you don't exactly take the time to apologize to the super uncool. But hey, I'll take what I can get. At least now Julian and I can go the lunchroom whenever we want (I hope). After overhearing her in the bathroom, I'm a little surprised when Stella begins her monologue. She recites the words I know so well in a quiet, flat voice, her gaze blankly focused on the auditorium's back wall. I mean, she has the speech memorized and everything, but it's not like she's really moving around or doing anything special. After all that bragging, her *Alice in Wonderland* is okay . . . but just okay. Could she actually have stage fright herself!? Still, the Sweets cheer loudly as she exits, her chin tucked down. I've decided my hands are too tired to clap.

As the lights come on and students are starting to stand up, Julian pokes me in the shoulder, "Yours was definitely the most unique!"

AFTER I GET MY MONOLOGUE GRADE BACK FROM MR. Diavolo the next day, I am pleasantly surprised to see an "A-" written onto the grading sheet. In his same shaky handwriting, the sheet says, *You went a little off-script . . . but the test of a true performer often lies in acts of bravery.*

Knowing Mr. Diavolo, he's probably quoting that from some weirdo play I've never heard of. When I think of him writing that sentence down and jiggling his eyebrows in a happy dance, though, it makes me smile.

As for Julian, it might still be winter, but he and I are already making a plan for next summer's Freeburger Pageant. Once we've got it planned out, we'll run it by Mr. Diavolo. Julian thinks it would be cool if we did a big group dance, and I agree. He even wants everyone to sing! Sometimes he comes to my house after school and we skip through song after song on my mom's computer, trying to decide on the right one.

He wants something more old-fashioned with violins. I want something with a big, heavy beat that will have the audience tapping their toes. Even though he rolls his eyes about it, I picture a whole crowd of kids, boys and girls, all doing the shimmy shake together.

"That would be pretty neat, right?" I ask Julian, and he just gives a sigh and rolls his eyes. He can be so high-maintenance sometimes.

But, whatever. I think I'll get my way.

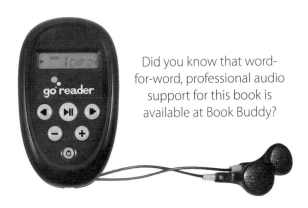

Did you know that word-for-word, professional audio support for this book is available at Book Buddy?

GoReader™ powered by Book Buddy is pre-loaded with word-for-word audio support to build strong readers and achieve Common Core standards.

The corresponding GoReader™ for this book can be found at: http://bookbuddyaudio.com

Or send an email to: info@bookbuddyaudio.com